finish

You need a dice, and a counter each.
Take turns to roll the dice.
If you roll 1, move 1 space.
If you roll 2, move 2 spaces, and so on.
The first player to get to the lighthouse is the winner.

This Clifford Annual
belongs to

....

....

....

My favourite dog is

....

Annual 2004

Contents

There's a super Clifford Annual competition at the end of the book. Why not enter? You might win one of the great Clifford prizes!

Based on the Scholastic book series CLIFFORD THE BIG RED DOG by Norman Bridwell.
Written and edited by Brenda Apsley and Jane Clempner
Designed by Julie Clough

Published in Great Britain in 2003 by Egmont Books Limited,
239 Kensington High Street, London, W8 6SA.
Printed in the U.A.E.   ISBN: 0 7498 5906 7

6

Clifford's Story

Once, not so very long ago, a little girl called Emily Elizabeth lived in the city. She wanted one thing more than anything else – a puppy of her very own.

Emily Elizabeth's mum and dad took her to see some new puppies. They were fat and cheeky – all except one.

He was very tiny, and much smaller than the others.

As soon as he saw Emily Elizabeth, he ran over to her, jumping and barking.

Emily Elizabeth chose the little red puppy because even though he was tiny, he had a big heart. He had kind eyes, and Emily Elizabeth loved him from the moment she stroked his soft puppy fur and held him in her hands. She named him Clifford.

Clifford loved Emily Elizabeth, and Emily Elizabeth loved Clifford.

Emily Elizabeth's love made Clifford grow. She stroked him and patted him, and kissed his little black nose. She fed him and took him for walks and talked to him. And every day she told him how much she loved him.

And the more Emily Elizabeth loved
him, the more Clifford grew ...

He grew and grew ...

and grew ...

and
grew!

Clifford grew bigger
and bigger and bigger.
He grew until he was
bigger than Emily
Elizabeth's hand, and
bigger than Emily
Elizabeth. Soon he was
the biggest dog in the
whole wide world!
"WOOF!"

Clifford just kept on growing! He grew and grew until he was too big to fit inside Emily Elizabeth's house! He had to stay outside, and look in through her bedroom window. Emily Elizabeth felt sad. She knew that a special dog like Clifford needed a warm dog house to sleep in, and lots of space to run around in.

The city was no place for Clifford, so Emily Elizabeth and her family decided to find a new place to live. They packed up all their things in the car and drove away from the city. Clifford couldn't fit inside, so he went in a special trailer fixed to the back of the car!

Emily Elizabeth and her family drove to the coast, then they took a boat to Birdwell Island. Clifford liked it from the start, because it's in the shape of a dog bone!

Emily Elizabeth and her family made a new home on the island, in a big house with a big garden. Now Clifford has lots and lots of space to run around in, and a big dog house with his name over the door. Inside there's a big, blue Clifford-size bed, and stairs leading up to a platform so that Emily Elizabeth can get a friendly lick from her best friend.

Everyone on the island loves Clifford! "WOOF!"

Say Hello To Clifford's Friends

"WOOF!" says Clifford.
"I love it here on Birdwell Island! Life is SO much fun, and I have lots of great friends."

"Emily Elizabeth is the best friend a dog could have. She's smart and funny and lively – and I just love her!"

"This is **Cleo**. She's a purple poodle. She looks a bit fussy and fancy, but she's got a big heart. She's brave, and nothing scares her. She always tries to talk us into doing naughty things and having adventures. Cleo's a lot of fun!"

"**T-Bone** is a bulldog. He looks strong and tough on the outside, but inside he's really shy, kind and gentle. He's not the bravest dog in the world, and he doesn't like trying new things unless we help him. T-Bone's a big softie, and I like him that way!"

"Meet **Mum and Dad Howard**, Emily Elizabeth's parents. They're great!"

"**Charley** is Emily Elizabeth's best friend (after me, of course!). He lives with his dad, Samuel, on an old boat. He loves making music with pots and pans and things."

"**Jetta** is another of Emily Elizabeth's friends – well, most of the time! She can be a bit bossy and really likes to brag, but deep down, she's a good friend."

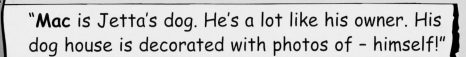

"**Mac** is Jetta's dog. He's a lot like his owner. His dog house is decorated with photos of – himself!"

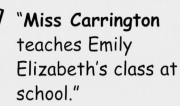

"**Miss Carrington** teaches Emily Elizabeth's class at school."

"**Laura** is Emily Elizabeth's cousin. She comes to visit with her dog, **Rex**."

"**Sheriff Lewis** is T-Bone's owner. He's a policeman, and the person who looks after things on the island."

"**Doctor Dihn** is the vet who takes care of all the animals on Birdwell Island – even me!"

15

Clifford's Dream

Emily Elizabeth had been to see the circus at Birdwell Park, and she couldn't wait to get home to tell Clifford all about it.

It was late when she got home, and Clifford was ready for bed. But Emily Elizabeth wasn't. She was much too excited to even think about going to sleep!

"Oh, Clifford, it was wonderful!" said Emily Elizabeth. "The park was full of stalls and rides, and there were balloons everywhere. The circus was in a big stripy tent called a Big Top. And you should have seen the fairy lights, and little flags."

Clifford yawned. He was very tired, and his eyes started to close.

But Emily Elizabeth didn't notice. "We had seats in the very front row. There was music, then a lady called a ringmaster came in to the ring. She said she was pleased to see us, and told us that the acrobats were coming on first."

Clifford was finding it hard to stay awake and he yawned again, but Emily Elizabeth took no notice.

"The acrobats did all sorts of jumps and tumbling, and at the end, the strong man lifted them up – one in each hand!"

Clifford was very, VERY tired. He yawned for a third time, and his eyes closed.

But Emily Elizabeth wasn't tired. She had lots more to tell him.

"Oh, Clifford, there was a little monkey wearing a blue jacket and cap. He did a funny dance, and he waved to Charley and me!"

Clifford was almost asleep, but that didn't stop Emily Elizabeth.

"And you should have seen the clowns, Clifford. Oh, they were so funny! One of them was carrying a big bucket of water, and he tripped, and the water went all over Charley and me. But it wasn't water – the bucket was full of tiny bits of paper! That made us laugh!"

By now, Clifford was fast asleep. ZZZZZZZZ!

Emily Elizabeth looked at him, and smiled. "Goodnight, Clifford," she said, kissing the tip of his big black nose. "Sweet dreams."

That night, Clifford had a dream ...

He dreamed that he went to the circus, too, with his friends T-Bone and Cleo.

When they got to Birdwell Park, it was full of people. But they didn't look very happy. There were no lights, and no music. The Big Top tent was dark and quiet, and the door flap was closed.

"WOOF!" said Clifford. He wondered what was going on.

"Sorry, but we can't do the circus show tonight," the ringmaster told them.

Clifford, T-Bone and Cleo looked at each other. They were very disappointed. "WOOF!" said Clifford.

The ringmaster explained. "The clowns and the acrobat and the jugglers were all coming by bus. But it broke down, and they won't be here in time. I hate to disappoint all these people, but we can't do a circus show without them, can we?"

Clifford had an idea. A wonderful idea! He took Cleo and T-Bone to a quiet corner.

"We can do a circus show!" he said to T-Bone and Cleo. "We know all about being acrobats and clowns, don't we? We play circuses all the time, don't we?"

"YIP!" said Cleo. "Yes – and we're good!"

"BOOF!" said T-Bone, who wasn't so sure. "Well, we can TRY, I suppose ..."

When they went back to the ringmaster, she smiled. She seemed to understood what they wanted to do. "You mean the three of you will do the circus show?"

Clifford nodded.
So did Cleo and T-Bone.
"WOOF!" said Clifford.

Soon, lights lit up the dark sky over the Big Top. The tent was full of music, and the audience were in their seats, waiting for the circus to begin.

The ringmaster stepped into the middle of the ring, and held out her arms.

"Welcome!" she said. "Ladies and gentlemen, I am pleased and proud to present, for one night only – Clifford's Amazing Circus!"

Clifford and his friends stepped into the bright spotlight, and the audience clapped.

"WOOF!" said Clifford.

Clifford the Strong Dog lifted up heavy weights as if they were balloons, then he lifted up the clowns' car. He even lifted up the ringmaster! The audience gasped, then clapped.

Cleo the Clown ran round and round the ring, and everyone laughed when Clifford dropped a giant custard pie on her.

When T-Bone the Brave stood on one end of the big see-saw and Clifford put his paw on the other end, T-Bone flew up into the air, turned one, two, three times ... then landed on Clifford's head!

"Hurray!" shouted the audience.

At the end of the show, Clifford and his friends took a bow. Cleo was on one of Clifford's ears, and T-Bone was on the other!

"Bravo!" said the people in the crowd, clapping and cheering. "Hurray for Clifford's Amazing Circus!"

"WOOF!" said Clifford. He thought it was the best fun ever!

In the morning, Emily Elizabeth still had lots more to tell Clifford about her visit to the circus.

But when she went to see him, Clifford was still fast asleep.

"Wake up, lazy bones," she said. "Why are you so tired?"

Clifford opened one eye. Didn't Emily Elizabeth know that it was hard work being a circus star?

Emily Elizabeth smiled, and shook her head. "Clifford," she said, "I think you've been dreaming!"

Dreams ...

What do you think Emily Elizabeth, Cleo and T-Bone are dreaming of? Draw lines to match them to their dream pictures.

Clifford's thought for today is:
"It's good to dream, because dreams can come true!"

What do you think Clifford is dreaming of? Draw and colour a dream picture for him. "WOOF!"

23

Count With Clifford

Clifford has lots and lots of friends.

"WOOF!" says Clifford. "One ... two ... oh, there are too many for me to count!"

Can you help him? Count the number of friends, and write a number in each box.

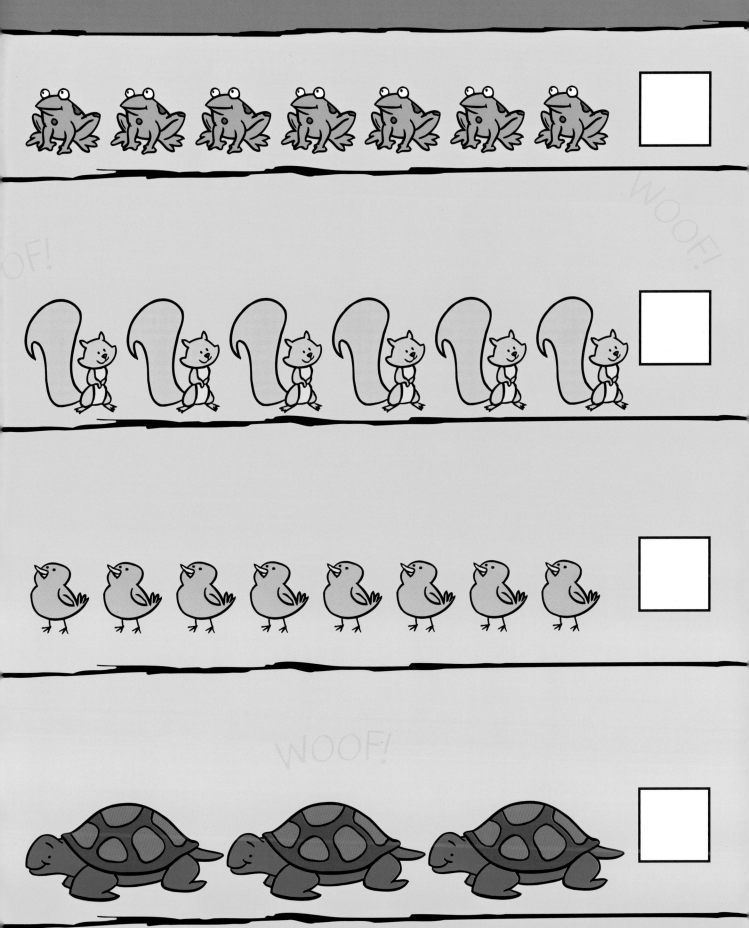

Emily Elizabeth's BIG Idea

Clifford loves going to meet Emily Elizabeth from school. And Emily Elizabeth loves to see her BIG best friend waiting for her.

One day, Clifford was waiting at the school gates, as usual. It was a lovely, sunny day, and he had brought his favourite stick so they could play fetch on the way home.

The classroom clock ticked and tocked. Suddenly the bell rang, and out ran the children.

"Clifford!" beamed Emily Elizabeth.

He gave her a big, happy lick, then fetched the stick for her to throw.

Emily Elizabeth shook her head. "Homework first!"

Clifford dropped the stick.

"Don't look sad!" said Emily Elizabeth, climbing up on to his back. "Tonight's homework is the best fun ever – and you can help!"

Clifford pricked up his ears.

"We've been learning all about the alphabet," explained Emily Elizabeth. "The letters make so many words!"

"WOOF!" said Clifford.

"We started with the letter **a**, and tomorrow it's the letter ..."

"WOOF!" said Clifford.

"You know it's the letter **b**, don't you?" laughed Emily Elizabeth. "Clever boy! My homework is to find interesting words that begin with the letter **b**."

Clifford ran to the bus stop.

"Very good!" laughed Emily Elizabeth. "But I have to find things I can take in to school. The best display wins a prize."

Back at home in the garden, the two friends began to search for things beginning with the letter **b**. There were lots of birds, but they flew away. There was Emily Elizabeth's bicycle, but it had a puncture. There were branches high on the tree and bushes that were too prickly, but nothing that Emily Elizabeth could put in her display.

Just then, Cleo and T-Bone came bounding in, and Emily Elizabeth told them about her homework. Without a thought, Cleo quickly found one of her bows and tied it on to Clifford's tail.

"**B** is for bow!" said Emily Elizabeth. "Thank you, Cleo. This is your prettiest bow, too, so it will make my collection beautiful – and that's another word beginning with **b**!" She gave Cleo a big hug.

T-Bone had run off, but now he was back, carrying his best bone. He dropped it at Emily Elizabeth's feet.

"For me?" she said, picking it up. "You're so kind! Look, Clifford, now I have a bow and a bone!"

But Clifford was looking sad. He wanted to help Emily Elizabeth, too. But he didn't have anything to give her.

Poor Clifford hardly slept that night. He tossed and turned, dreaming of things beginning with the letter **b**. But everything was too big – boats and buses and bridges and buildings!

On the walk to school the next day, Clifford felt quite miserable. But Emily Elizabeth didn't. She skipped along, carrying her bow and her bone. "Come on, Clifford, cheer up!" she said. "I had the best idea last night. You wait and see!"

Clifford looked at her.

"Will you stand outside school for a little while today?" she asked. "And when I whistle, will you look in through the window?"

Now Clifford looked puzzled. But he would do anything for Emily Elizabeth. She was his best friend.

Inside the classroom, Emily Elizabeth stood next to the window and waited.

Miss Carrington came in. She looked at all the displays, then she noticed Emily Elizabeth standing by the window.

"What's this, Emily Elizabeth?" she asked.

"My collection of things that begin with **b**," said Emily Elizabeth proudly. She held up her things. "**B** is for bone and bow ... and beautiful. But my favourite word beginning with **b** is ..." She gave a loud whistle, and Clifford's face appeared at the window. "BIG!"

"WOOF!" said Clifford, and everyone laughed.

"And there's one more thing starting with **b** that I could never do without," she added. "My best friend!"

"WOOF!" said Clifford, and everyone clapped.

"Well done, Emily Elizabeth!" said Miss Carrington. "You win first prize for finding the best collection of words that

start with **b**! And here's something starting with **b** that you can have lots of fun with!" She handed Emily Elizabeth a smart new pair of binoculars.

"WOOF! WOOF!" cheered Clifford.
"See you after school, boy!" waved Emily Elizabeth.

Birdwell Island

BAY OF BIRDWELL

That day, Clifford was the happiest dog on Birdwell Island – something else that starts with **b**!

Alphabet Fun

Emily Elizabeth's class have been learning to write the letters of the alphabet. Can you help by filling in the letters they have missed out?

a _ c d

_ l m _ o

_ u v

Draw a circle around the letter that starts your name.
How many other things can you think of that begin with the same letter?
Draw your favourite in the box!

f h i j

q r s

x y

Clifford's BIG idea for today is:
"Friends always help each other!"

WOOF!

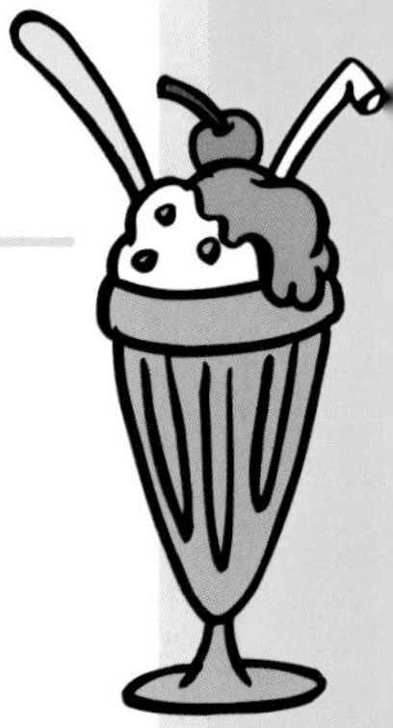

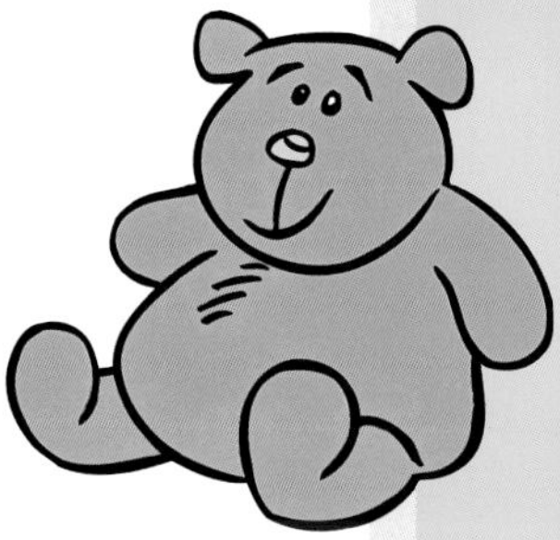

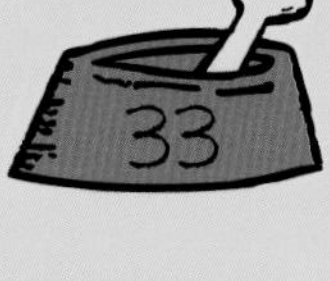

Clifford's New Friend

Summers are hot on Birdwell Island. One day, Clifford gave Emily Elizabeth and Charley a ride to the pier so that they could cool off.

Emily Elizabeth and Charley bought trays of chips and sat on a bench. They were happy just chatting and looking at the ocean.

But Clifford had other ideas. He wanted to be IN the ocean, so he ran to the end of the pier, jumped over the rails – and landed in the sea with a big splash!

"WOOF!" said Clifford. Being in the sea was fun!

He splashed so hard that the water went up into the air, and – SPLASH! – all over Charley and Emily Elizabeth!

"Hey!" said Emily Elizabeth. "I'm all wet!"

"Whoa!" said Charley. "So am I!"

"WOOF!" said Clifford.

Clifford showed Emily Elizabeth and Charley how he shook himself dry, so they tried it.

"Hey, this is fun!" said Emily Elizabeth, shaking her hair from side to side.

34

Clifford was paddling around in the sea when he felt a tap on his back leg.

"Onk, onk!" said a grey seal.

"WOOF!" said Clifford. He wondered what the seal was doing there.

The seal dived under the water, then came up again. She looked at Clifford, then swam a little way off, and waited.

"Onk, onk!" said the seal.

Emily Elizabeth and Charley watched from the pier. "I think she's trying to show you something, Clifford," said Charley.

"Yes," said Emily Elizabeth, "she wants you to follow her."

Clifford understood. "WOOF!"

Clifford paddled after the seal. Charley and Emily Elizabeth went after them, walking along the beach.

The seal swam into shallow water and stopped at some rocks.

"Onk, onk!" she said, holding up her flipper.

Clifford looked. There, hidden in the rocks, was a tiny seal pup! It looked very sad.

"WOOF!" said Clifford. He could see that the seal pup was stuck. A big wave had pushed him on to the rocks, and he was too small to get back into the water.

Just then, Emily Elizabeth and Charley arrived. "He's only a baby," said Charley, "and he looks very weak. What shall we do?"

"I know!" said Emily Elizabeth. "Do you remember last summer, when that baby whale got washed up on to the beach? Dr Dihn helped him. She knew what to do."

"Yes, I remember," said Charley. "She put him in a paddling pool in the garden, and looked after him until he was well again."

"WOOF!" said Clifford. He remembered how he had taken him back to the ocean so that he could swim back to his family again.

Clifford carried the seal pup to Dr Dihn's house. She looked after him until he was well again. She fed him lots and lots of fish!

"WOOF!" said Clifford when he went to visit him. He had grown, and now he was almost as big as his mother!

Dr Dihn laughed. "Yes, Clifford," she said. "He grew and grew, just like you!"

Soon it was time for the seal pup to go back to the ocean.

Clifford carried him into the water.

"WOOF!" he said, giving him a gentle nudge with his nose.

The little seal was very pleased to be back in the water. He dived and jumped and swam in circles, weaving in and out of Clifford's legs.

"WOOF!" said Clifford, splashing around after him. Playing with his new friend was good fun!

Clifford and the seal pup were still having fun when the mother seal arrived.

"Onk, onk!" said the mother seal.

"Onk, onk!" said the pup.

"WOOF!" said Clifford, wondering what that meant.

"It means hello," said Emily Elizabeth.

The seal and her pup dived and leapt again, then they swam out into the deep water.

"Onk, onk!" they said, looking back at Clifford.

"That means goodbye," said Emily Elizabeth.

"Onk, onk!"

"And that means thank you, Clifford."

"WOOF!" said Clifford.

Clifford's BIG idea
for today is:
"Be a good friend."

Hot Diggity Dog

Hot diggity dog! Clifford just loves visiting the hot dog cart, because he just loves hot dogs! He can eat ten!

Hot Diggity Dog

Look carefully at the pictures. They look the same, but there are 8 things that are different in picture 2. Can you find them all? Say "WOOF!" each time you find one, and circle it with a pencil if you like.

HOT DOG CART

Hot Diggity Dog

Big, Bigger, Biggest

Emily Elizabeth loved Clifford so much that he grew and grew and grew. He grew into a big dog, then an even bigger dog, then the biggest dog in the whole wide world!

Draw a circle around the biggest in each set, and tick the smallest.

Good Idea, Clifford!

This is a story in words and pictures. Listen to the story, then look at the pictures, and tell the story in your own words. Remember to "WOOF!" just like Clifford!

1

One day, Clifford and Charley go to the pier, where they meet Jetta. She doesn't look very happy. "I'm going home!" she says. "The roundabout is broken!"

"WOOF!" says Clifford. He loves the ocean. He likes to go for a paddle in the water every day. He jumps in off the end of the pier – SPLASH!

2

44

3

Charley looks around. "There are lots of people on the pier," he says. "They'll all be disappointed if they can't have a ride on the roundabout."

Charley puts his head on one side. He always does that when he has a problem to sort out. "I wonder if there's anything we can do to help?" he says.

4

5

"WOOF!" says Clifford, and he stops paddling so that he can think about it, too. Then he has an idea. A good idea. A VERY good idea!

"WOOF!" Clifford jumps as high as he can. He jumps out of the water, over the rails at the end of the pier, and lands – THUMP! – on the wooden floor.

6

Clifford makes the pier roll from side to side. Then it shakes and rocks to and fro, just like a fairground ride. "WOOF!" says Clifford.

7

"Whoa!" says Charley. He goes backwards and forwards, and from side to side. "Great idea, Clifford. This is much more fun than a ride on the roundabout!"

8

I Spy

Clifford likes going to the library with Emily Elizabeth. But he's MUCH too big to fit inside, so he has to wait outside for her. When Clifford gets bored, he looks in through the windows and plays a game of I spy. You can play, too. Look at the picture and say the name of something that starts with each letter sound.

WOOF!

WOOF!

WOOF!

WOOF!

WOOF!

WOOF!

"I spy with my little eye, something beginning with ... **b**."

"I spy with my little eye, something beginning with ... **t**."

"I spy with my little eye, something beginning with ... **w**."

"I spy with my little eye, something beginning with ... **ch**."

"I spy with my little eye, something beginning with ... **sh**."

WOOF!

Dogs And Owners

Can you match these dogs to their owners? Draw a dog lead from each dog's collar to its owner's hand, and say the names. If you need help with the names, pages 14 and 15 will help you. The first one has been done for you!

50

Clifford To The Rescue

When the fair came to Birdwell Island, Jetta was first in line to ride on the big ferris wheel.

"Shall I ride with you?" asked Emily Elizabeth. "We can hold hands if it gets scary."

Jetta shook her head. "No way!" she said. "Riding two in a cab is for scaredy cats only. I'm not scared! I'm going up on my own!"

When the owner pressed a button, the big ferris wheel started to turn. Jetta's cab moved up, higher and higher and higher, until it was right at the top of the wheel.

Then it moved down the other side, lower and lower and lower, until she was close to the ground again. Jetta waved to Emily Elizabeth. "This is fun! Look – no hands!"

Round and round went the ferris wheel, up to the top, down to the bottom, and right up to the top again. But then – CLANG! CLUNK! – the wheel stopped moving!

Jetta looked out, and her eyes opened wide. It was a long, long way down.

The wind blew, and Jetta's cab swayed backwards and forwards so that she had to hold on to the sides. "Ooh, I feel ill!"

When Jetta looked down again, there was a crowd of people staring up at her.

"The engine is broken!" the owner called. "Don't worry. We'll get you down soon."

"HOW?" said Jetta. "Oh, I wish I had someone to hold hands with. And what if I'm still up here when it gets dark, and there are bats and things flying about? Oh, HELP!"

The owner couldn't fix the engine. He was going to ring for the fire engine when Emily Elizabeth spoke to him.

"I know how we can get Jetta down," she said. "My dog Clifford's very tall. He can reach her!"

"WOOF!" said Clifford.

Clifford stretched up to the top of the big wheel. "WOOF!" he said, moving his collar so that Jetta could hold on to it.

Jetta's eyes opened wide. "Are you joking?" she said. "What if I fall?"

"WOOF!" said Clifford. He wanted Jetta to know that she could trust him.

Jetta held on to Clifford's collar, and he lowered her, down, down, until her feet touched the ground again.

"You can have a free ride when I fix the wheel," said the owner.

"Are you kidding?" said Jetta. "I never want to see this thing again."

As Jetta ran off, Emily Elizabeth turned to Clifford. "And she didn't even say thank you!"

A few minutes later, Jetta called out from behind the ice cream van. "Here, Clifford!" she said.

What a surprise! Jetta had bought Clifford the biggest ice cream sundae you've ever seen.

"Thank you!" said Jetta.

Clifford's BIG idea for today is: "Have respect."

"WOOF!" said Clifford.

Clever Clifford

Clifford's so big that he can juggle big fat pumpkins as if they are tiny little pingpong balls!

He can bounce them on his nose ...

on his head ...

and from one ear to the other!

Clever Clifford!
Clever YOU if you can count all the pumpkins on these pages!
Off you go: 1, 2, 3 …

Clifford's Big Sneeze

This is a story in words and pictures. Listen to the story, then look at the pictures, and tell the story in your own words. Remember to sneeze just like Clifford!

Clifford and his friends T-Bone and Cleo just love rolling in the grass. The thicker and smellier the grass is, the better they like it!

1

They love jumping into piles of dry leaves, too. They make great crinkly, crackly sounds. One day Clifford makes himself into a slide for Cleo and T-Bone.

2

3

When T-Bone stands on Clifford's head, he looks worried. "Is it safe?" he asks. "What if I fall?" Cleo gives him a little push. "Oh, go on!" she says.

T-Bone jumps off Clifford's head, and slides down his neck, faster and faster. Then he shoots down Clifford's back, to the end of his tail – and up into the air!

4

5

T-Bone lands – crinkle, crackle! – in the pile of leaves. "Wow!" he says. "That was brilliant. Let's do it again – but with a MUCH bigger pile of leaves this time."

Clifford, Cleo and T-Bone collect the crinkliest, crackliest leaves they can find: brown leaves and gold leaves and orange leaves and red leaves.

6

They build the leaves into a big, BIG pile. It's almost finished when some dust goes up Clifford's nose. "Oh, no," says Cleo. "He's going to ..."

ATISHOO!

What happens next? Draw and colour a picture of Clifford's big sneeze.

Wish-Bone Day

One fine morning on Birdwell Island, there was excitement in the air. Clifford and his friends were at the lighthouse. There was going to be an announcement!

"T-Bone has asked us all here today," began Emily Elizabeth, "because today is Wish-bone day!"

"Woof!" said T-Bone, pulling himself up as tall as his little legs would allow.

"What's Wish-bone day?" asked Charley. "It sounds cool!"

"Wish-bone day," explained Emily Elizabeth, "is the anniversary of the day T-Bone buried his magic wish-bone. On this day, and this day only, we can hunt for the buried bone, and whoever finds it can make a wish."

"And will that wish come true?" asked Charley.

T-Bone nodded proudly.

"That's really cool," said Charley. "Come on, race you to the beach!" But then he stopped. "Wait a minute," he said, turning back to T-Bone. "If you buried the magic wish-bone, then surely you know where it is!"

T-Bone looked embarrassed.

"Well, not really," explained Emily Elizabeth. "T-Bone buried it five years ago, and although he's looked for it every year since then, he's never found it!"

"Never mind," smiled Charley. "This makes the hunt more fun! Let's split up, and meet back here later."

Everyone rushed off in different directions, imagining what they would wish for if they were lucky enough to find the magic wish-bone.

Cleo wanted to be a famous film star ...

T-Bone wanted to be
Super-T, and save
the world ...

Emily Elizabeth wanted to
be the world's best basketball
player and win a giant
trophy ...

Charley wanted to be
a pirate, and sail the
stormy seas ...

And Clifford wanted to dive
into the biggest ice-cream
anyone had ever seen!

But after a short time, they were all back at the lighthouse.

"It's not much fun looking for things on your own," said Emily Elizabeth.

Everyone agreed.

"Let's team up then!" said Charley. "We'll pretend we're pirates searching for treasure!"

Emily Elizabeth ran home and found some paper and handkerchiefs to make pirate hats. Charley borrowed his dad's telescope, and T-Bone used his crayons to draw a wish-bone treasure map. It wasn't a very good map, in fact T-Bone didn't know which way up to hold it, but he could pretend!

Soon they set off, with T-Bone as their captain and
Clifford as their giant pirate ship! They travelled by land
and by sea, braving whatever dangers came their way. They
peered over the tallest trees and spied across the rooftops.
Along the beach they sailed, round the playground, past the
school, to the end of the pier – and back again.

But there was no sign of the magic wish-bone, and now it
was starting to get dark.

"I think your wish-bone is safe for another year," sighed
Charley. "But my wish came true anyway!"

"And we had the most fun ever!" added Emily Elizabeth.
"Let's play again tomorrow."

T-Bone nodded. He couldn't wait to lead the wish-bone
hunt again.

Everyone set off happily for home.

Emily Elizabeth was racing to catch up with Clifford when she remembered that she had left her pirate hat on the beach. She ran back to the rock in the sand where she had left it, but when she looked more closely at the rock, she realised it wasn't a rock at all – it was the magic wish-bone!

She held it tightly in both hands and looked up to where the stars were twinkling. "I wish that my friends and I can always be as happy as we have been today," she said. Then she carefully put the wish-bone back, and covered it with sand. She had a feeling that her wish really would come true.

T-Bone's Treasure Map

Can you find the way through the maze to the treasure chest?
What things do you pass on the way?

T-Bone has buried lots of bones.
How many of each colour can you
find? Count, and write the
number in each box.

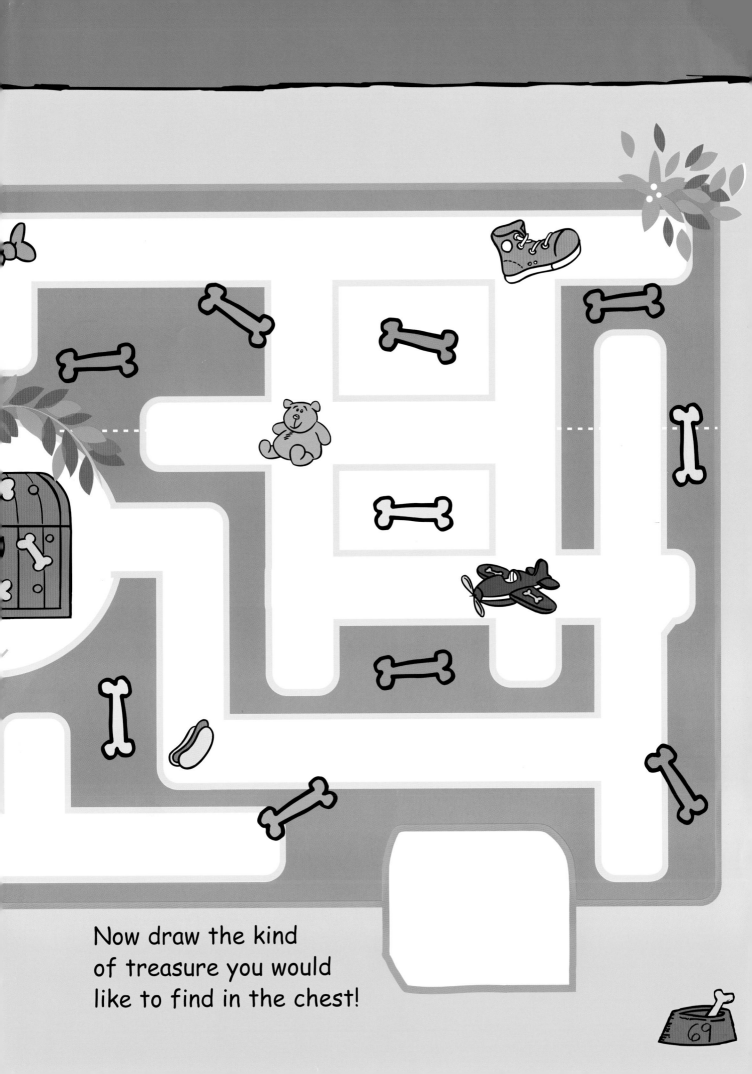

Now draw the kind
of treasure you would
like to find in the chest!

COMPETITION

It's competition time ...
and we have some fabulous prizes
for you to win, courtesy of Character Options.

1st Prize

The **First Prize** winner will receive
a big, yes **really** big, 70cm Clifford.
Suitable for 18 months +.